Little Kangaroo
Finds His Way

A Little Animal Adventure

Little Kangaroo
Finds His Way

Written by Ariane Chottin
Adapted by Patricia Jensen
Illustrations by Catherine Fichaux

Published by The Reader's Digest Association Limited
London ❖ New York ❖ Sydney ❖ Montreal

One summer in Australia, it was so hot that plants and grasses died and the river dried up near the kangaroos' home. They didn't have enough water or food.

'We're in danger,' said Grandfather Kangaroo. 'One of us must go to the Wise Lizard. She'll know what to do.'

'But who will go?' asked Grandmother. 'We are all needed here to take care of the babies and to search for something to eat and drink.'

Mother Kangaroo spoke up. 'I think my son is old enough to make the trip.' She turned to Little Kangaroo and asked, 'Will you go for us?'

Little Kangaroo nodded and tried to look brave.

Little Kangaroo set off and hopped across the hot plains until he came to the edge of the deep forest. 'I want to help my family,' he thought, 'but I'm scared. What if I get lost?'

He tried to remember the directions he had been given but the heat had made his head feel funny. 'The Wise Lizard lives somewhere beyond the forest,' he said to himself.

Then, Little Kangaroo saw a path through the trees. He took a deep breath, went into the forest and wondered where the path would lead.

Little Kangaroo followed the path through the forest. On the far side, he found flat, open land. First he hopped in one direction. Then he tried another direction. He didn't know where to go.

'Yoo hoo!' called a large owl. 'Do you need some help?'

'Yes,' said Little Kangaroo. 'I must find the way to the Wise Lizard. It's very important.'

'You're quite young to be making such a long trip,' said the owl. 'I will help you.' The owl nodded to his left. 'Go in that direction until you come to a stream.'

Little Kangaroo followed the owl's advice. Finally, he reached a wide stream and sat down at the edge of the water.

'I don't know where to go next,' he thought. Tears filled his eyes as he looked up and down the stream. 'I'm lost!' he cried.

'Zzzzzzzz. Where are you going?' buzzed a large, fuzzy bee.

'I'm looking for the Wise Lizard,' said Little Kangaroo. 'I need her advice.'

'You're very young to make such a long trip,' said the bee. 'I will help you. The Wise Lizard lives on the other side of the stream.'

'But how will I get across?' asked Little Kangaroo. 'The water looks too deep.'

'I'll show you the best place to cross,' said the bee. 'It's easy.'

Following the bee's directions, Little Kangaroo leapt across the stream.

'Where are you going in such a hurry?' asked a bright green caterpillar.

Little Kangaroo explained, 'I have an important question to ask the Wise Lizard.'

'The Wise Lizard!' said the caterpillar. 'I've always wanted to see her, but I could never travel that far. My legs aren't long and strong like yours.'

'I'll carry you,' offered Little Kangaroo. 'And you can show me how to get there.'

'I think I know the way,' said the caterpillar. 'Let's try it.'

The new friends crossed a wide, grassy valley. The caterpillar looked around and began to worry.

'I'm afraid we're lost,' he said. 'I thought the Wise Lizard would be here, but I don't see her anywhere. Do you?'

'I don't see anything except those two fat baobab trees,' said Little Kangaroo.

'Baobab trees!' said the caterpillar. 'This is the right place! I know the Wise Lizard lives somewhere near two big baobab trees.'

A few minutes later, Little Kangaroo shouted excitedly, 'Do you see that?'

Sitting on a high rock was the Wise Lizard. Little Kangaroo joined the other animals standing near the rock.

The Wise Lizard noticed the young kangaroo right away. 'Where have you come from?' she asked in a kind voice.

'From far, far away, where the river has dried up,' said Little Kangaroo. 'We're running out of food and water. I'm here to ask for your advice.'

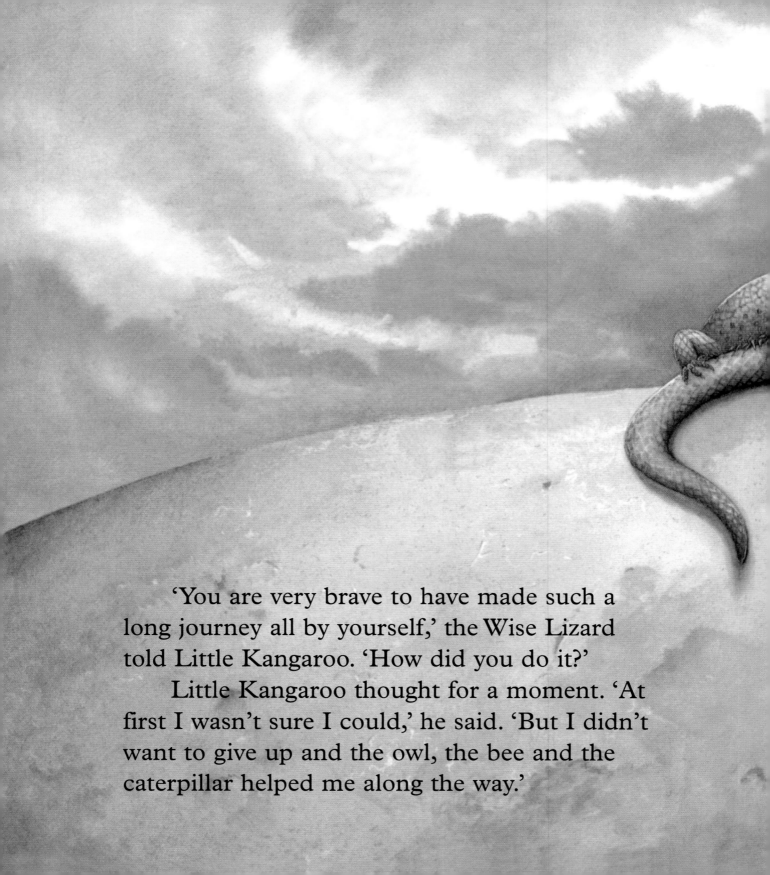

'You are very brave to have made such a long journey all by yourself,' the Wise Lizard told Little Kangaroo. 'How did you do it?'

Little Kangaroo thought for a moment. 'At first I wasn't sure I could,' he said. 'But I didn't want to give up and the owl, the bee and the caterpillar helped me along the way.'

The Wise Lizard nodded. 'You've done very well,' she said. 'So take this advice back to the other kangaroos. Tell them to walk towards the mountains until they come to a large lake. There they will find enough water and food.'

Little Kangaroo thanked the Wise Lizard and carried his friend the caterpillar back to the stream. Then Little Kangaroo hurried all the way home.

'Look who's here!' shouted the other kangaroos. They gathered around Little Kangaroo, happy to see him safe and sound.

'I knew you could do it,' whispered his mother. 'And now you know it, too.'

As the sun rose early the next morning, the kangaroos set out to find their new home. They all hopped along merrily, but no one felt more joy than Little Kangaroo.

All about ... KANGAROOS

LEAPING AROUND
The kangaroo moves from place to place by jumping. It can often cover 3 metres in one leap! Its powerful tail is used for balance.

SAFE AND SNUG
Kangaroo babies, called joeys, are tiny at birth. A joey continues to grow in its mother's pouch for the first few months of life.

FACT FILE
LOOK-OUT DUTY
Kangaroos live in groups. When the group is busy grazing, one kangaroo will keep watch and thump the ground to alert the others to danger.

Did you know?

FISTICUFFS
Kangaroos are skillful fighters. They fight by grabbing or pushing with their forepaws and kicking with their hind legs.

RUNNING ON EMPTY
Kangaroos can go for long periods of time without drinking. Some kangaroos live without water for two or three months!

MUNCHIES ...
Kangaroos are grazers. They eat mostly grass and some plants. Like sheep, they chew their food for a long time before swallowing.

Little Kangaroo Finds His Way is a Little Animal Adventures book
published by Reader's Digest Young Families, Inc.

Written by Ariane Chottin
Adapted by Patricia Jensen
Illustrations by Catherine Fichaux
Notebook artwork © Paul Bommer

This edition was adapted and published in 2008 by
The Reader's Digest Association Limited
11 Westferry Circus, Canary Wharf, London E14 4HE

® Reader's Digest, the Pegasus logo and Reader's Digest Young Families
are registered trademarks of
The Reader's Digest Association, Inc.

We are committed both to the quality of our products
and the service we provide to our customers.
We value your comments, so please do contact us on
08705 113366 or via our website at
www.readersdigest.co.uk
If you have any comments or suggestions about the
content of our books, email us at
gbeditorial@readersdigest.co.uk

Printed in China

Book code: 637-040 UP0000-1
ISBN: 978 0 276 44367 1
Oracle code: 501800111H.00.24